DON'T WEAR

Polka-Dot Underwear

WITH WHITE PANTS

(AND OTHER LESSONS I'VE LEARNED)

DON'T WEAR

Polka-Dot Underwear

WITH WHITE PANTS

(AND OTHER LESSONS I'VE LEARNED)

BY ALLISON GUTKNECHT

ILLUSTRATED BY STEVIE LEWIS

ALADDIN

NEW YORK   LONDON   TORONTO   SYDNEY   NEW DELHI

This book is a work of fiction. Any references to historical events, real people, or real places are used fictitiously. Other names, characters, places, and events are products of the author's imagination, and any resemblance to actual events or places or persons, living or dead, is entirely coincidental.

ALADDIN

An imprint of Simon & Schuster Children's Publishing Division

1230 Avenue of the Americas, New York, NY 10020

First Aladdin paperback edition November 2013

Text copyright © 2013 by Allison Gutknecht

Illustrations copyright © 2013 by Stevie Lewis

All rights reserved, including the right of reproduction in whole or in part in any form.

ALADDIN is a trademark of Simon & Schuster, Inc., and related logo is a registered trademark of Simon & Schuster, Inc.

Also available in an Aladdin hardcover edition.

For information about special discounts for bulk purchases, please contact Simon & Schuster Special Sales at 1-866-506-1949 or business@simonandschuster.com.

The Simon & Schuster Speakers Bureau can bring authors to your live event. For more information or to book an event, contact the Simon & Schuster Speakers Bureau at 1-866-248-3049 or visit our website at www.simonspeakers.com.

Cover designed by Jessica Handelman

The text of this book was set in Arno Pro.

The illustrations for this book were rendered digitally.

Manufactured in the United States of America 1013 OFF

2 4 6 8 10 9 7 5 3 1

Library of Congress Control Number 2013944030

ISBN 978-1-4424-8393-4 (hc)

ISBN 978-1-4424-8392-7 (pbk)

ISBN 978-1-4424-8394-1 (eBook)

For Mom and Dad,
WHO TAUGHT ME SO MANY LESSONS
(UNFORTUNATELY, JUST NOT THE ONE ABOUT
THE POLKA-DOT UNDERWEAR)

Many Thanks to

ALYSON HELLER, CHARLIE OLSEN, AND THE TEAMS
AT ALADDIN AND INKWELL FOR UNDERSTANDING
THE IMPORTANT THINGS IN LIFE: GUMMY BEAR
FLAVORS, PRESIDENTIAL PAGEANT RIVALRIES,
AND A WELL-PLACED "WAHOO!"

Contents

CHAPTER 1

The Trouble with White Pants

I KEEP TELLING MOM ABOUT THE WHITE PANTS, and she says to wear them anyway.

"They will make me fall down," I explain.

"Pants do not make you fall down, Amanda," Mom answers, because she does not understand anything at all.

"Yes, they do." I stomp my foot and cross my arms and put on my very best "I am pouting now" face. "White pants like dirt, and they will make me fall in it."

"Then be extra careful at recess, please," Mom says, holding the awful pants open for me to step in.

"No."

Mom sighs a big gust of breath in my face and stares at me with her "I mean business" eyes. "Amanda Berr, I am going to count to three."

"I will get ketchup on them," I say.

"One . . ."

"I will drop marker on them," I say.

"Two . . ."

I groan like a dinosaur and lift up one leg just so Mom will stop counting.

"Here is a deal," I begin. "I will wear these awful white pants if you buy me periwinkle pants." My favorite color is periwinkle. It is more beautiful than blue and more perfect than purple and it is a fun name to say. But I do not have one piece of periwinkle clothing, and I think this is

unfair. I checked my whole entire closet—shirts and shorts and dresses and ugly fancy blouses that Mom keeps in plastic until Easter. No periwinkle. I had held my periwinkle crayon from my box of 152 colors up to each piece, just to be sure. And still nothing.

"I'll look for some," Mom says, shaking the white pants in front of me.

"Today," I insist. "I want periwinkle pants today."

"I cannot get you periwinkle pants today," Mom says. "Why can't you just like a nice, normal color—like pink? How about if I get you pink pants?"

"I hate pink."

"Good, *these* pants aren't pink." Mom shakes the pants even more ferociously.

I grab the pants in my own two hands then. "I will dress myself. I am not a baby," I say.

"Fine," Mom answers. "Be downstairs and dressed in five minutes, Amanda. And in *those* pants. I don't have time for any more funny business today."

So I stuff my legs into the pants and stomp down to the kitchen table, and Mom does not even say, *Thank you for wearing the awful white pants, Mandy.* Mandy is my real name even though Mom thinks it is Amanda. I do not like the name "Amanda" because it does not have any *Y*s in it, and this is a tragedy. I like to make *Y*s with curlicue tails and I cannot do this when there are no *Y*'s in my name, so this is why my name is Mandy and *not* Amanda.

"Finish up your cereal, Amanda," Mom says. "Your bus will be at the corner in ten minutes. Hurry."

"I cannot hurry because of these pants," I tell her.

"Don't be ridiculous," Mom responds, which I think is pretty rude, if I am being honest.

"I am being serious," I insist. "If I eat quickly, I will dump the cereal onto the pants and they will be dirty because white pants love dirt. I told you so already." I lift one kernel of cereal onto my spoon very slowly and raise it toward my mouth, just to show Mom how careful I have to be.

"If you want to eat that way, it's up to you," Mom says. "But you only have five more minutes to do so, Amanda."

"Mandy," I remind her, but she does not correct herself. Mom is not such a good listener. She was not such a good listener ever, but she is even worse now that the twins are here. Everything in this house for the past five months has been about the twins:

"The twins are hungry."

"Don't be noisy, you'll wake the twins."

"Aren't the twins adorable?"

The twins are not adorable. They're damp. "Damp" is my new favorite word—my teacher, Mrs. Spangle, taught it to us during our science lesson. It means when something is just a little bit wet. And the twins are always just a little bit wet. Their diapers are wet or their drool is wet or their food is wet. They're damp. Like that washcloth that is still damp the next morning even though it's had the whole entire night to dry from your bath. And damp things are gross, I've decided.

Mom says it's not nice to call the twins "gross." She says I have to call them "Samantha and Cody," but most of the time, she's not paying enough attention to see if I do, so I don't.

My little brother Timmy also hardly gets any attention anymore, but I don't mind that so much. Because he's pretty gross too.

"Oof, Cody is wet again." Mom pats the diaper on one of the twins and lifts him up. He starts to wail then, because all the twins like to do is cry and get even damper.

They are pretty terrible, if I am being honest.

"Amanda, can you get yourself to your bus stop?" Mom calls over her shoulder on her way to the twins' room.

"I'm eight," I answer, because Mom forgets that I am not a baby. I know important things like how to get to my bus stop and how to read books without pictures in them and how to cook—well, to pour cereal, which is pretty much the same thing.

"Don't forget your lunch box!" Mom calls from the twins' room. "It's on the counter." I swirl the rest of my cereal around in the bowl and try to splash a little on my pants so I can change them. "Hurry, Amanda!"

I groan like a dinosaur again and pick my

Rainbow Sparkle lunch box up off the counter. Rainbow Sparkle is who I want to be when I grow up: She is fast and she is funny and she has purple eyes, which is what I want to have (hers are almost periwinkle, only not quite). I'm stuck with brown eyes and brown hair, when all I want are beautiful purple eyes and silky white hair like Rainbow Sparkle's.

Rainbow Sparkle is a cat, if I forgot to mention. She has her own show on TV.

"You can't become a cartoon cat when you grow up," Mom always says. She really does not understand anything at all.

"I'm leaving!" I yell to Mom as I head for the front door. On my way I see my stuffed Rainbow Sparkle sitting underneath the coffee table, and I cram her into my lunch box even though one of Mrs. Spangle's rules is "No toys in school." I am going to need Rainbow Sparkle to protect me from these pants. Because Rainbow Sparkle is the only white-colored thing in the whole universe that is not awful.

Mrs. Spangle looks like a porcupine, but she is nicer. Porcupines stick people with their quills and Mrs. Spangle has red hair that looks like quills, but she does not stick people with it. I know this because I touched Mrs. Spangle's hair once and it did not stick me. It did feel a little bit prickly at the top, but it was soft when I rubbed my hand over it.

"Please don't pet me, Mandy," Mrs. Spangle had said, so I have not touched her hair again, even though sometimes I would like to.

I am thinking about petting Mrs. Spangle's hair while she stands at the front of our room and tells us about our big second-grade Presidential Pageant.

"The president's coming?" I call out.

"Mandy," Mrs. Spangle says with a warning in her voice. Mrs. Spangle has seven big rules for our classroom, and I am pretty good at following three of them. "No calling out" is number four on the list, and that is not one of my favorites.

I cover my mouth with one hand and shoot the other one in the air.

"Yes, Mandy?" Mrs. Spangle calls on me.

"The president's coming?"

"That's a good guess, but no," Mrs. Spangle answers. I slide down in my chair and slouch, disappointed. "Instead of having one president visit, you're all going to become presidents for the day!"

And I hate to say it after I made the big deal with the slouch and all, but this is just about the best news I've ever heard.

"Wahoo!" I leap up from my chair and pump

my fist in the air. Luckily, three other kids do this too, except without the "wahoo."

I sit back in my chair and raise my hand as quickly as I can. I place my left hand over my mouth, just to remind myself to keep it closed until Mrs. Spangle calls on me.

"Yes, Mandy?" Mrs. Spangle says, so I snap my left hand away from my mouth.

"Can I be George Washington?" George Washington is clearly the best president because he was first, and I always like to be first. I was born first in my family, so it only seems fair.

"I'll be assigning your parts for the assembly next week," Mrs. Spangle says. "In the meantime, we're going to get caught up on our presidential knowledge each day, so you'll all get to learn about the presidents who might not be as famous as George Washington or Abraham Lincoln."

I shoot my hand into the air again.

"Yes, Mandy?"

"I would like to be George Washington, please," I say. I use "please" and everything, because that is one of Mrs. Spangle's rules that I am good at: "Be polite."

"Everyone will find out next week," Mrs. Spangle says. "Now let's get our things and line up for lunch. Natalie's table first." Natalie's table always gets to be first because Natalie sits with her hands folded all the time and she makes her whole table do the same. Natalie is no fun at all, if I forgot to mention.

When it is finally my table's turn, I grab my Rainbow Sparkle lunch box out of my cubby and stand behind Anya. We walk in a not-so-straight line to the cafeteria, and I plop my lunch box on top of the table so that it makes as loud a noise as possible. Natalie gives me a dirty look and covers her ears, but Anya slams her lunch box on the table right next to mine, even louder than I did.

Anya is my favorite person in the world, at least most of the time.

I like Anya because both "Amanda" and "Anya" begin with the letter *A* and end with the letter *A*, which is kind of amazing. Of course, Amanda has another *A* in the middle, so my name is a little better, but Anya's is pretty good too. (And Anya gets to have a *Y* in her name all the time, which makes me a little bit jealous.)

Plus, Anya likes being loud and she likes Rainbow Sparkle's TV show, so we have a lot to talk about.

"Do you know Dennis hid my lunch box in the cubbies again?" Anya asks. Dennis sits next to Anya in Mrs. Spangle's class, and she has a lot of problems with him because he is horrible.

I look over at the boys' cafeteria table and

glare at Dennis. Dennis has a Mohawk in his hair and so many freckles on his nose that you can barely see it at all.

"Leave Anya alone, Freckle Face!" I yell at him, but he doesn't hear me. That is probably for the best, because another one of Mrs. Spangle's rules is "No name-calling." But Freckle Face is just such a perfect name-call for Dennis.

Though I've always kind of wanted to have some freckles myself, if I am being honest.

Anya shrugs. "Don't worry about him," she says. "I'll tell Mrs. Spangle if he does it again, and then he'll have to miss recess."

Recess. Recess is the best time ever. Anya and I have been playing Squash the Lemon on the slide with some other girls, which is not really allowed because the lunch aides think we are going to squash each other to death, but we play until they blow the whistle about it.

I open my lunch box very carefully so that Rainbow Sparkle does not fall out. If Natalie sees her, she will tell Mrs. Spangle about it because Natalie is the police of Mrs. Spangle's rules. I give Rainbow Sparkle a quick pat on the nose so she does not feel left out, pull out my food, and then slam my lunch box shut real quick.

"Shh." Natalie gives me a not-nice look through her glasses, and I give her my best "You are driving me bananas" face. Dad taught me the "You are driving me bananas" face, but I do it better than him, I think.

I unwrap my sandwich and find peanut butter and jelly, which is my favorite. Except this sandwich has strawberry jam, and I keep telling bad-listener Mom that I hate strawberry jam because it has seeds. I like grape jelly only, because grape jelly is purple, which is almost like periwinkle. Plus, no seeds.

Also, jam is slippery and slimy, and now I have these white pants and I can't get any strawberry on them.

"Ugh," I groan real loud so my whole table can hear.

"What's wrong?" Anya asks. I point to my sandwich and make a face.

"Oh no, seeds," she says, and this is one reason why Anya is my favorite person in the world.

I bite into my sandwich as neatly as possible, making sure to hold the whole thing over the table and not over my pants. It takes a very long time to eat this way. So long that I don't even have a chance to eat my carrot sticks, but I didn't want to eat them anyway, so this is not a tragedy.

I always tell Mom that I want gummy bears in my lunch instead of carrot sticks, and she says this is not possible because gummy bears are not healthy. But gummy bears taste like fruit and they are delicious, so I do not know what the big deal is.

I line up behind Anya to hit the playground, and when we are allowed to go outside, I make a beeline for the slide. Three other girls from our class are already waiting at the bottom of the slide's ladder, ready to play our not-allowed game until the lunch aides come out of the cafeteria.

"Let's go, let's go, hurry!" I call. Everyone starts climbing to the top of the slide. The first girl slides down the normal way and plants her feet firmly in the dirt at the bottom. The next girl gets into position at the top, hanging each of her legs off either side of the slide. When she reaches the bottom, she slams into the first girl and they both grunt. And this is why Squash the Lemon is the best recess game ever.

Natalie slides down the same way, and then Anya. I am next.

"Do *not* go fast, Mandy," Natalie calls back to

me. "I can hardly breathe." Now, this makes no sense at all, because the whole point of Squash the Lemon is to go fast and squish people. So I start making my way to the top of the ladder so I can give them all the biggest slam they've ever had.

"Ready or not, here I come!" I call from the top of the slide, and I decide to go extra fast just for Natalie.

"Ewww!" I hear behind me. "Ewww!" I turn around and see Dennis and three of his silly boy friends standing at the bottom of the ladder.

"What do you want, Freckle Face?"

"Ewww, I can see your underwear," Dennis says. "Ewww!"

I was not expecting this.

I quickly feel around the back of my pants, making sure that the band of my underwear is not peeking out the top. It is not.

"Liar!" I yell at Dennis.

"Mandy wears polka-dot underwear," Dennis says in a singsong voice, and if I were not standing at the top of a slide right now, I promise I would tackle him.

Especially because I'm pretty sure that I *am* wearing polka-dot underwear.

How does he know that?

"Mandy wears polka-dot underwear," Dennis repeats. "You can see it through her pants."

All this commotion breaks up the squashing of the lemons at the bottom of the slide, and Anya and the other girls come around to see why Dennis is yelling. Anya looks up at me, and her eyes grow as wide as pancakes. She motions for me to get off the slide, real small so Dennis can't see.

I look down the ladder but decide that the slide itself is my fastest way off. So I shimmy to the bottom, which isn't even very fun because there is no one to squash. Anya is there to meet me.

"You can see your underwear through your pants," she whispers to me. "I think it's the sun." Anya hurries me off to stand under the oak tree in the shade, somewhere my polka dots will stay hidden.

And at this moment there are three things that I am furious at: Dennis, Mom, and these awful white pants.

Anya gives me her sweater to wear over my bottom for the rest of recess, and this is another reason why she is my favorite person in the world. When we get back to our classroom, I stuff my lunch box into my cubby and pop right up to Mrs. Spangle's desk before she can say I am not allowed.

"I need to tell you a secret," I say quietly.

"Not now, Mandy," Mrs. Spangle says. "It's time for—"

"It's an emergency," I interrupt her. "Emergency" is the kind of word that gets grown-ups to listen to you. "Broken" and "stain" and "dropped on his head" are also good words for this, I've learned.

"What is it?"

"I need to take off my underwear." I whisper this sentence real quietly in Mrs. Spangle's ear, and I think I spit on her a little bit.

"What do you mean? Did you have an accident?"

I shake my head. "My mom made me wear these awful white pants, and so everyone can see my underwear." I say this part super whispery too. "Dennis saw them on the playground."

"Stand back a second," Mrs. Spangle says, so I follow her directions and take one step back, because I am very good at listening to Mrs. Spangle's "Follow directions" rule. "Don't worry, I can't see anything."

"Look harder," I say, taking another step back, which means I have to talk a little bit louder. "What do you see now?"

"Nope, nothing," Mrs. Spangle answers. "You're safe."

I take one more step back, just to make sure. "Are you absolutely positive you can't see my underwear? They're polka dot." I accidentally say this real loud because I forgot about my super-whispery voice. And who appears at Mrs. Spangle's desk right at this moment but Dennis, and he laughs.

"I promise, Mandy," Mrs. Spangle says. "Take a seat, please, and get ready for math. Dennis, you too." Mrs. Spangle gives him a look like he is in trouble, but she does not write his initials on the board, which I think is unfair. If I had laughed about Dennis's underwear, I am abso-lutely positive I would have gotten my initials on the board, so I stick my tongue out at him.

"Hey, Natalie," Dennis says as he sits down. "Did you know Mandy is wearing polka-dot underwear?"

"So?" is all that Natalie answers. And sometimes I am very happy that Natalie is so dull. Because boring people do not care about things like polka-dot underwear.

I sit at my desk, but I keep Anya's sweater tied around my waist for the rest of the afternoon, and Anya does not even complain once that she is cold.

This is why I like Anya almost as much as I like Rainbow Sparkle and almost as much as I like fruity gummy bears. I could eat a gummy bear or twenty right now. Because gummy bears never, ever come in polka dot.

CHAPTER 2

Gummy Bears

IF I'VE LEARNED ANYTHING, it's that a girl needs an emergency stash of gummy bears hidden in her room at all times, especially after a whole day of wishing she had gummy bears in her lunch box and finding crummy old carrot sticks instead.

Gummy bears are my favorite food in the world. Gummy snakes are okay too, I guess, if you like snakes, which I do not. But I like bears. Sometimes I pretend that my last name is "Bear" even though it's "Berr." I am supposed to say it like,

Brrrr, it's so cold outside, but that is just boring. So I like to tell people our name is "Bear," and this makes my parents annoyed. I am not sure why they have to care so much.

A good place to get gummy bears is from a grandmom, because a parent will usually say "No." But grandmoms are pretty nice about gummy bears if you ask real sweetly, with a big hug and kiss. Grandmoms love to be kissed, so I kiss mine a lot whenever I want a bag of gummy bears. And—ta-da!—here they are.

I like to squeeze a gummy bear between my thumb and index finger until the head gets real big and then I rip it off with one bite. Red ones are my favorite, but that's only because they don't make periwinkle gummy bears yet. I eat my gummy bears like a rainbow—orange, yellow, green, blue—but I save all the red ones for last because they are the best.

I am sitting here all by myself after school biting heads off of gummy bears because Mom is feeding the twins or changing the twins or doing something else that is damp with the twins. And they're not being very quiet about it either. They are howling, actually. Or one of the twins is howling, and I don't care which one it is, except I'd like to know which one I have to tackle later.

Mom says I'm not allowed to tackle the twins, of course. And I don't, except for in my mind.

Timmy would come eat gummy bears with me if I asked him, but he is only three years old, and I cannot be seen hanging out with a preschooler. That would just be humiliating.

I get up off my bed and place my bag of gummy bears by my feet gently, because I do not want to lose any bears. I grab one corner of my Rainbow Sparkle bedspread and pull and pull like I am playing tug-of-war. I pull until the whole bedspread is on the floor in a heap, which is a pretty big job. Then I lift up two corners and toss the whole thing into the air: This is how I create my Magic Mountain Wonderland. Around the mountain I stack the pillows from my bed until they form a fence, and then I sit in the middle. No one knows about my Magic Mountain Wonderland but me, and that is just the way I like it.

I hold the gummy bear bag in my lap and start placing the bears one by one into the holes on the mountain. I put some of the green bears in a hole at the bottom of the mountain, because they like grass. I place the blue bears in a long, windy hole that looks like a river, because they like water. And I let the red bears live at the very tippy-top of the mountain, because they are the best.

"Amanda!" Mom calls up the stairs. "What are you doing?"

"Reading!" I yell back, even though I am not. If I say "reading," my parents think I am being good and leave me alone, I've learned. Sometimes I really am reading, because I like to read, but mostly I like to read books about Rainbow Sparkle. And I've read all those already.

Mom doesn't know yet that she ruined my life with these white pants, and I don't even think she would care because I am not a twin. I know I am better than the twins, though, so that is something. At least I don't use a diaper. Even Timmy still wears a diaper when he is sleeping, so I call him a baby and then Mom tells me to go to my room. This is why it is very, very important to have gummy bears in my bedroom at all times—I am sent here a lot.

"Go play in the backyard with Timmy. It's a beautiful day," Mom calls.

"No, thank you," I say. I am not going to be seen in public with a three-year-old. No way!

"Let's go, Amanda," Mom calls again. "I'm not asking, I'm telling."

I tried to say this to Mom once—"I'm not asking, I'm telling"—and she was not pleased, so I don't know why she gets to say it to me.

I crinkle up my bag of gummy bears as softly as I can, but I groan as loudly as I can so Mom can hear it. I slide one of the pillows surrounding

Magic Mountain Wonderland like it is a gate and then shut it behind me. I slam my bedroom door closed so that no one will come in, and I pound my feet down the stairs super loud, and when one pound comes out too softly, I go back up the step and do it again.

"Knock that off," Mom says. "Samantha and Cody are falling asleep."

I stomp toward the back door just a little bit more quietly and am about to slam the door behind me when I think better of it. I don't want to hear those twins cry again either. Instead I stand right outside the kitchen window, turn my back to it, and point to my bottom.

"What do you see?" I yell loudly, so Mom can hear through the screen.

"Shh." She shushes me again. "What's the problem now?"

"What do you see?" I repeat. My back is still to

the window, but I'm sticking my bottom up in the air so she knows what I am talking about.

"Oh my . . . ," Mom begins, and then she starts to laugh. Which I think is pretty rude, if I am being honest.

The harder Mom laughs, the angrier and angrier I get. Timmy jumps off the swing to see what is so funny, so I tell him to mind his own beeswax, which at least makes Mom stop laughing.

"Don't talk to your brother like that," Mom says. "And from now on, no more white pants. I promise."

So at least this polka-dot underwear got me something good, I guess.

I do not play with Timmy, but I do let him swing on the other swing with me, which I think is pretty generous.

"Push me, Mandy," he says, but I ignore him because I am not going to be bossed around by a preschooler. I am first, just like George Washington, so I am the boss. I am the president of the Berr family, I think.

I get tired of swinging because the sun is shining right into my eyes and Mom will not buy me the fancy-dancy periwinkle sunglasses that I want. I jump off of the swing and walk over to the sandbox, picking up a large twig on my way.

"Where you going, Mandy?" Timmy calls after me. He is a big pest sometimes.

"I cannot see without fancy-dancy periwinkle sunglasses!" I yell back to him, and this answer makes him be quiet because he does not understand big-kid things like sunglasses.

I pull off the lid of the sandbox, which is shaped like a turtle. The lid is supposed to be its shell, but it is all green, which is not very turtlelike at all. With my hand, I flatten out a whole side of the sandbox so that the sand is super smooth, just like paper. Then I lift up the twig and very carefully write *President Mandy Berr* in large letters across the sand. I give the *Y* an extra big curlicue and even draw a sun face in the middle of the curl. I stand back to admire my work.

"Abracadabra!" Timmy dives into the sandbox, and sand flies everywhere—out of the turtle and onto my ankles, ruining my very first presidential signature with the sunshine curlicue.

"TIMMY!" I scream so loud that it tickles the back of my throat. Timmy tries to scramble out of the sandbox like a beetle stuck in the bathtub, his sneakers scraping against the bottom of the turtle.

"What's going on out there?" Mom calls out the kitchen window.

"Timmy ruined my presidential signature!" I stomp my foot and cross my arms and put on my "I have never been so angry in my life" face, because I have never been so angry in my life.

"I think it's time you two came inside anyway," Mom says. "Put the lid back on the sandbox, please." Mom disappears from the window.

"You do it, Bigfoot," I tell Timmy, even though I know that I am much stronger when it comes to turtle lids. I scuff my shoes across the grass until I reach the back door and bang inside.

"Where's my lunch box?" I ask.

"Where you left it," Mom answers. "Not on the counter, which is where I asked you to put it."

"Humph." I shuffle into the living room, and I find my book bag and lunch box next to the front door, right where I had thrown them. I kneel down and pop open my lunch box so that I can bring Rainbow Sparkle upstairs to play in my Magic Mountain Wonderland. Because Rainbow Sparkle is the only one in this whole family who understands that I am the president.

CHAPTER 3

Caterpillars

IT HAS BEEN A WHOLE WEEK, and Mrs. Spangle still has not told me that I can play George Washington in the Presidential Pageant.

She has taught us about a bunch of other presidents who are not nearly as important as George Washington. I have not learned much, really. All I know is that President Taft was very round, and President Clinton played the saxophone, and President Garfield got shot, which is a pretty big problem, so I hope Mrs. Spangle doesn't get confused and make me play him.

But I have even more bad news, and that is that Dennis has a name-call for me now, when my whole point was only to have one for him. He calls me "Polka Dot." Anya says this is not so bad—it could be "Underwear," she points out, because Anya is helpful like that. But I would prefer Dennis have no name for me and I could just call him "Freckle Face" whenever I felt like it.

"At least you only wear polka-dot underwear sometimes, right?" Anya asks. "Dennis has those freckles all of the time." Though, to tell you the truth, I'd really like to ask Dennis how he got those freckles so I could get some for myself. But I never, ever talk to Dennis in a nice way.

Also, I will never be wearing polka-dot underwear again thanks to Dennis, which makes me kind of sad, because I do love polka dots and I am pretty sure they were my lucky pair. But now they make me feel kind of embarrassed and hot on the forehead.

Mom keeps telling me to play outside with Timmy after school, which is no fun. Even when I tell her I want to read, she shoos me out the door and says I need "fresh air." Mom is always telling me not to be fresh, so I don't know why the air is allowed to be.

Timmy looks nothing like me, I think, so I like to pretend that he is not my brother at all. He has blue eyes, and blue eyes are much closer to Rainbow Sparkle's purple eyes than my brown ones, so this makes me mad. I'd like to have blue eyes too, and sometimes I wonder if there is a way I can steal them from Timmy.

"Push me, Mandy?" he asks.

"No," I answer, because I am the boss. But I do not feel like swinging or running or going in the sandbox myself, so I decide that I am going to pretend I like Timmy just for today and let him play Squash the Lemon with me on our slide. I will even be the anchor at the bottom so that Timmy can squash me, which I think is pretty generous because squashing is the best part of the game.

"Come here," I tell him. "I am going to let you play my favorite game."

"Yippee!" Timmy pops off the swing as fast as a preschooler can pop and walks over to the slide.

"I am going to slide down first," I explain. "Then you are going to slide down after me like this." I climb up the ladder, which is not nearly as high as the one on the playground, and show him how to slide down with his legs hanging off both sides of the slide. "You got it?"

"Got it!" Timmy says. I climb back up the slide and go down the regular way, which is a very boring way to slide. Timmy climbs up the ladder behind me, drapes his legs over each side of the slide, and slithers down. He bumps into me when he reaches the bottom, and it barely hurts at all, which is not fun in this case.

This is the problem with playing Squash the Lemon with a three-year-old, especially when there is only one of them.

"You need to go much faster, or else this game is no fun," I explain. "I will show you." I sit him at the bottom of the slide real tight so I can slide into him. Then I climb up the ladder, drape my legs over the sides, and slide down at my fastest speed ever.

And I knock Timmy off the slide and into the grass.

And then he cries, because he can't even take a little squashing.

"I'm going to tell Mommy," he says, so I call him a baby and walk to the side of the house to be by myself.

The side of our house is a little bit spooky. Not spooky like Halloween or anything, but it has some weeds and some cobwebs and a lot of dead leaves. No one ever goes to the side of our house but me. I don't even like it that much, but it is better than nothing.

There are always a lot of bugs here. I do not love bugs, but I do not hate them either. I look along the bricks on the side of my house to see if there is anything interesting. One time I found a bird's nest lying next to it, but with no eggs inside, which was less exciting (and plus, Mom wouldn't let me touch the nest because she thought I would get a disease).

I walk along the side slowly, trying to put on my best scientist eyes like Mrs. Spangle talks about during our science lessons. It is not sunny here, so at least I do not need the fancy-dancy periwinkle sunglasses that Mom won't buy me. I run the fingers of my left hand along the house to see if anything feels different. There is nothing for a long time, and then suddenly, my hand hits something furry.

When I feel it, I scream a little bit.

I step closer to look, and I see a hairy, crawly caterpillar making its way along the house. A real-life caterpillar! Mrs. Spangle just taught us about caterpillars last month, about how they turn into butterflies and all that fantastic magic business. But she would not let us touch the ones that she kept in our classroom terrarium. This is my big chance.

Carefully, I place my right hand in front of the caterpillar's head so he can crawl onto it. He does! I pull my hand away from the wall, and his teensy hairs tickle the top of my hand like a feather. I feel his top with my other hand, and he is squishy, almost like a gummy bear.

And I kind of want to squeeze him, just to see what will happen. Not real hard or anything—just a little bit. Like a gummy bear before you bite the head off.

I put my thumb and index finger around the middle of the caterpillar and bring them together slowly.

"Amanda!"

I am so startled that I twitch my hands fast and the caterpillar falls off. Which is just terrible, because now I have to go digging through dead leaves if I ever want to find him again.

"You made me drop my caterpillar!" I yell at Mom.

"Why did Timmy come inside crying?"

"You made me drop my caterpillar!" I yell again, just in case she did not hear what a great tragedy this is. She is a bad listener, after all. "I was just about to squeeze him."

"Squeeze him? Amanda, you cannot squeeze caterpillars. You will kill them. Is that what you want?"

I think about this for one second only. "Is that the truth?"

"Yes, Amanda," Mom says.

"Mandy," I correct her, because she never, ever remembers.

"Fine, now get inside, please, *Mandy*, and apologize to Timmy." And I do not like how she says the *Y* version my name at all because it is in her mean "Go to your room, Amanda" voice. So maybe I should let Mom call me "Amanda," but only when I am in trouble so that "Mandy" is not ruined.

"How do you know it's me who made him cry?"

Mom gives me her "I know everything you do" look and stares at me down the point of her nose.

"Okay, fine," I say. "Will squeezing caterpillars really kill them?"

"Yes," Mom answers. "Plus, you could get a disease."

"I won't squeeze them again," I promise. But only because I don't want them to die, not because of the disease part.

"Sorry, Timmy," I call as I run through the back door. I trot up the stairs to my bedroom, open the pillow-gate to my Magic Mountain Wonderland, and place my bag of gummy bears on my lap. I take out a red one and pinch it between my thumb and finger, then I stick it in my mouth.

And don't tell Mom, but I do not even wash my hands first.

CHAPTER 4

George and Me

THE NEXT DAY MRS. SPANGLE MAKES Natalie and me be reading partners, which is almost as horrible as being reading partners with Dennis. Natalie is very serious, and I am very not serious. She never calls out or has her initials on the board or gets a warning from Mrs. Spangle.

Plus, Natalie thinks that she is a better reader than me, and that is just a lie.

I slump down in the Reading Corner next to Natalie. "I'll read first," I say.

"No, you went first last time," Natalie says. "It's my turn." Natalie is very into turns, and I am very into going first. She opens the book to the place where we had left off. It is a story about President Lincoln, but I learned everything there is to know about Abraham Lincoln way back in kindergarten, so this story is not interesting to me.

"'President Lincoln delivered the famous Gettysburg—'"

"How about if we read something different?" I interrupt Natalie's reading.

"We're supposed to read this," Natalie argues.

"But Mrs. Spangle will never know if we just—" I look behind me at the books stacked up in the Reading Corner, which all look much more interesting than this silly Lincoln book (plus, I bet they have many more pictures)—"read this one." I pick a book off the shelf, and I don't even care which one it is just as long as it is not about some silly speech.

"No," Natalie says. "We have to read this." And this is why Natalie and I are not friends.

I slump back down next to her and rest my elbows on my knees and my chin in my hands. Natalie's glasses are framed in black, which seems like a waste. If I were lucky enough to wear glasses, I would make sure the frames were a stand-out-and-shout color like periwinkle, or at least red.

"Can I try on your glasses?" I interrupt Natalie's reading again.

"No," she answers.

"Just for one single second?" I ask. "Please?" I am super polite, just like Mrs. Spangle's rule, because even black glasses are better to try on than no glasses at all.

"No," Natalie says again. I sigh so that she knows I am not pleased, but Natalie just keeps reading this Abraham Lincoln book. Natalie reads with no expression and I read with a lot of expression, but Natalie won't let me read one word before it is my turn.

"There is an exclamation point there," I interrupt her again. "At the end of that sentence. You did not read it."

"You don't read punctuation, Mandy," Natalie says, like I am some kind of dope or something.

"I *know*." I say "know" real loud because Natalie is making me angry. "But you have to exclaim when you say it. Like this." I try to pull the book out of Natalie's hands to demonstrate.

"It's not your turn!" Natalie holds on tight to the sides of the book and lets out a big exclamation point.

"See how you did that?" I say. "You made an exclamation! Like, 'Wahoo!'" I am a very helpful reading partner, I think.

"I'm telling." Natalie stands up in a huff and a puff and marches off toward Mrs. Spangle's desk.

Natalie is a big tattletale.

Mrs. Spangle tells Natalie and me to stop reading together, which is the best news I've heard all day. She does not tell me that I will be George Washington in the assembly, though, which would have been even better news.

When we are packing to go home, Mrs. Spangle

has the Paper Passers hand out sheets to take to our parents. "Make sure your moms and dads see this as soon as you get home," she says. "It's their invitation to our Presidential Pageant." And this is my big chance.

I shoot my hand in the air, following the "No calling out" rule and everything.

"Yes, Mandy?" Mrs. Spangle calls on me.

"Do I get to be George Washington?" I ask.

"I haven't assigned parts yet," Mrs. Spangle says. "Later this week."

"Don't make Polka Dot George Washington," Dennis says when Mrs. Spangle isn't paying attention.

"Stop it, Dennis," Anya says, because she is my friend and Dennis is not.

"Yeah, stop it, Freckle Face," I echo. "You don't know anything." And Dennis pets his Mohawk and sticks his tongue out at me.

When I get home, I put the invitation for the Presidential Pageant in front of Mom's nose right away so she cannot miss it. I know if I wait too long, Timmy or the twins will start crying and she will forget. So I hold the paper way high up so it touches the tip of her nose and is right in front of her eyes.

"Are you trying to give me a paper cut?" Mom takes the sheet from my hand and pulls it away from her face.

"You need to put this on your calendar right now," I say. "Mrs. Spangle says so."

"A Presidential Pageant," Mom reads. "That sounds exciting. I'll mark down the day."

"And no twins allowed," I say. "And no Timmy, either."

"Timmy will be in preschool," Mom says. "And I'll have Grandmom babysit the twins. Don't you worry about a thing."

"Good." I nod with satisfaction.

"Who are you playing in the assembly?"

"George Washington," I answer, even though I am not sure that this is true. Because if I am not George Washington, I am not going to show up at all.

One of the twins starts crying then, of course, because they do not know how to do anything else. Mom groans, and I wonder if she thinks the twins are annoying too. "Be right back," she tells me. "Then I want to hear all about your part."

Mom leaves the kitchen and heads for the twins' bedroom, and I am alone again. Which is better than being with Timmy or the twins, I guess.

I walk around the kitchen saying, "I cannot tell a lie" over and over with all kinds of expression to see what sounds best. I decide I might as well practice my George Washington part now, so that I am ready when Mrs. Spangle finally tells me that I am playing him in the assembly. I try to roll the sides of my hair into curls like he did, but it does not look right because my hair is straight and brown and not white like George's. Even if I do not like white on pants, I like it on hair because it reminds me of Grandmom and Rainbow Sparkle.

I cannot pretend to be George Washington with no white hair, so I open the sugar container on the counter and tap some sugar on top of my head. I study my reflection in the oven door, and I look a little better, so I run back and tap on another handful. And then I decide that I should stop before—

"What do you think you're doing?!"

—Mom finds me.

"Being George Washington," I answer, which I am pretty sure Mom should know by looking at me. "I cannot tell a—"

"Amanda," Mom says. "I am going to count to three."

I know then that I am about to get sent to my room. At least I still have half a bag of gummy bears and my Magic Mountain Wonderland there waiting for me.

CHAPTER 5

Gymnastics Champion, Only Not

IT IS VERY, VERY HARD TO GET SUGAR out of hair, I've learned. Because sugar is sticky and it gets slimy when Mom pours water over my head, and this sticky gook only makes Mom redder in the face.

It is Mom's fault, though, about the sugar, because she went to the twins' bedroom when I was talking about my George Washington part and she did not listen to me much, so I do not even feel too bad about the whole thing.

I am not allowed to watch Rainbow Sparkle's

show on TV for a whole week now, which is a much worse punishment than sitting in my room with gummy bears, so I am pretty unhappy. Plus, my hair is kind of sticky.

"Touch my hair," I say to Anya the next morning at school, because I want to see if my hair still feels like a sucked-on lollipop.

"Why?"

"Because it is sticky," I say.

"Ew, I don't want to feel it, then," Anya answers. "It looks shiny, though."

"Really?" I had not looked at my hair much since my bath except to make sure it was not white anymore (because I did not want Dennis to come up with another name-call for me when I only have one for him).

"Mm-hmm," Anya answers, so I decide it is okay that my hair is sticky as long as it is shiny, too. Because everybody knows that shiny, sparkly hair is the best kind, even if it does feel like old candy.

Natalie sits next to me in the cafeteria and tells me not to unwrap my sandwich so loudly, and this is ridiculous because there is no way to unwrap a sandwich quietly. At least Mom made my sandwich with grape jelly today, which tastes so much better than that seedy strawberry stuff.

I take a bite of my sandwich, and a big glob of jelly shoots out of the bread and lands with a splat on the cafeteria table. I mop it up with one finger and stick it in my mouth because I do not want to waste one bit of no-seeds jelly.

"Ew," Natalie calls. "You can't eat off the table. It has germs."

"It was not on the table long enough to get any germs," I tell her. "And also, it is none of your beeswax."

"You are probably going to get a disease,"

Natalie says, and I am positive that Natalie would not touch a caterpillar, which is why Natalie and I will never be friends. "Here, you can use my napkin to wipe up the rest."

"I don't need your silly napkin," I say. "I have a perfectly good finger." I slide my finger against the table and pop the rest of the jelly into my mouth.

"Yuck," Natalie says. "That is disgusting." And I do not even answer her because Natalie doesn't understand why you should never waste grape jelly.

The lunch aides are standing by the slide when we get to the playground, which does not seem like a very nice thing to do.

"No more Squash the Lemon," they say. "Someone is going to get hurt."

"What are we going to do now?" I ask Anya.

"Let's go see what the other girls are doing,"

Anya suggests, and we walk over to the grassy part of the playground, where I try never to play. Usually the girls who play here do only "Miss Mary Mack" and "Down by the Banks" and other hand-clapping games, and they are no fun at all, especially because I can never remember where to put my hands.

Of course, Natalie plays here almost every day.

"What are you guys doing?" Anya asks.

"Gymnastics," one of the girls answers. "The three of us are in the same gymnastics class, so we're practicing."

"That's dumb," I say to Anya. "The playground does not even have a trampoline." The trampoline is the only thing I ever did when I had to go to a gymnastics birthday party. You cannot bounce up and down on the grass like you can on a trampoline because grass is not very jumpy.

"Oooh, what kind?" Anya asks the other girls.

I forgot that Anya took gymnastics when she was little, but then she stopped because she ice-skates now.

"We were doing forward rolls," one of the girls says. "But now we're doing cartwheels."

"I love cartwheels," Anya says, and before I can blink, she throws her hands on the ground, sticks her feet in the air, and turns in a circle.

Anya can do a lot of things, I guess.

The three other girls from the gymnastics class do cartwheels too. And then Natalie gets ready to do one.

"Natalie, you better let me hold your glasses so you do not break them," I tell her, and I hold out my hand to take them. I am sure Natalie cannot do a real cartwheel, and so she will probably crack her glasses in tiny pieces. I am very considerate, I think.

"No, thank you," Natalie says, and before I

can say one more thing about the glasses, she does a perfect cartwheel and her glasses do not even fall off. And if Natalie can do a cartwheel, I do not see why I shouldn't be able to do one too.

"Stand back, everybody," I say, because I want to make sure everyone is paying real close attention. "My turn."

"Do you even know how to do a cartwheel?" Natalie asks.

"Of course I know how to do a cartwheel," I say, even though I have never actually tried one. But I am sure I can do one if Natalie can, with her glasses on and everything, so I am not too worried.

I take a deep breath, lift my arms in the air just like Anya did, and roll to my right.

And next thing I know, I am on the ground.

This is not how this cartwheel was supposed to go.

Worst of all, the other girls are laughing, which does not seem very nice to me. Even Anya is laughing, so I do not take her hand when she reaches it out to help me stand up.

This is why Anya is my favorite person in the world *most* of the time and not *all* the time.

Because she knows how to do a cartwheel. And because sometimes she laughs at me, and that is a pretty rude thing to do.

The lunch aides blow the whistle then, and I am happy to hear it even though I usually hate that whistle sound. I cannot believe that I do not know how to do a cartwheel and Natalie does. This is a real tragedy—a big, humongous tragedy that I must fix immediately.

CHAPTER 6

A Dumbbell by Any Other Name

ONCE WE HAVE SETTLED DOWN FROM RECESS, Mrs. Spangle says, "I am going to assign your parts for the Presidential Pageant." I have to uncross my arms then, even though I am still angry, because I cannot let out a "Wahoo!" with my arms crossed.

I sit at my desk super-duper straight, and I even fold my hands like Natalie because it looks very presidential, I think.

"I want everyone to remember that all of the parts for this assembly are important," Mrs.

Spangle says. "Even if you do not receive the role you had hoped for, I want you to work very hard at learning your lines so you are the very best president you can be." And I wish Mrs. Spangle would just hurry up and tell me that I am George Washington already.

I tap my toes against the floor and wiggle my fingers on the desk because I am nervous and jumpy. I would like to see my lines right away, but Mrs. Spangle is taking her time picking up an enormous pile of papers from her desk.

"These are your scripts," she explains. "I've highlighted your lines in yellow marker so you can see where your part is. I'm going to call your name, and when I give you your script, you can flip through to find your section. Anya." She hands Anya a thick pile of stapled pages, then she does the same for ten more people who are not me.

"Dennis," she calls, and Dennis takes his script and flips through it quickly.

"Yes, Teddy Roosevelt!" He shoots his fist in the air. "Mustache, here I come!"

"No calling out, please," Mrs. Spangle reminds him, and I am shaking so much with excitement now that I think I am going to fall over.

"Mandy," Mrs. Spangle finally says, and she hands me my very own script with *Mandy Berr* written at the top. Not *President Mandy Berr*, which I would have liked better.

I move the pages around quickly and look for the words "George Washington." I see many yellow marks across the lines, but no presidential names—only the word "Narrator" where the name "George Washington" should be.

"Who is President Narrator?" I ask.

"No calling out, Mandy," she says.

I raise my hand but Mrs. Spangle does not

call on me, even though this is an *emergency*.

"Now that you all have your scripts in front of you," she begins, still ignoring my hand, "let's go over who is playing whom." I wave my hand back and forth in case she cannot see it.

"First, Mandy is going to be our narrator," Mrs. Spangle continues, motioning for me to lower my hand. "She is going to introduce all of our presidents to the audience."

I shoot my arm in the air again.

"Yes?" she calls on me.

"I am supposed to be George Washington," I explain, and I feel tears tickling the back of my eyes.

"The narrator is going to be a great part for you. You'll see," Mrs. Spangle says. "Now, who's next? Follow along in your scripts."

Natalie raises her hand.

"Right, Natalie, tell everyone your part."

"George Washington," Natalie answers.

My chin drops and my eyes widen into huge pancakes, and I push on them with my fingers to make the tears stop tickling. Because I am absolutely positive that this is the worst news I have ever heard in my life.

Mrs. Spangle is my least favorite person in the world. I am even angrier with her than I am at anyone else, and I am angry with a lot of people right now.

Making Natalie George Washington in our Presidential Pageant is the worst thing that Mrs. Spangle could have done—Natalie, who does not know how to exclaim or to make her hair white or to be the first at anything. Natalie knows how to do a cartwheel, but that is not going to get her very far in being the best George Washington ever, which would have been me. I am positive that Natalie is not the president of her family like I am the president of mine.

I am stuck being the narrator, and I don't even know what the narrator is, but it is not a president, and so I am very, very upset. I think Mrs. Spangle felt a little bad because she called me to her desk and told me that the narrator has the biggest speaking part of anyone in the show. And that she knows that I read with expression, so this is why she gave the part to me. And that the narrator is the storyteller who holds the whole assembly together.

But the narrator is not a president, and this is the problem that Mrs. Spangle is missing.

And the narrator is really, really not George Washington.

And George Washington is Natalie. Natalie! That is almost as bad as George Washington being Dennis—maybe even worse, because at least

Dennis knows how to exclaim. Dennis gets to be Teddy Roosevelt, which is also terrible, because he will get to wear a fake mustache and I have always wanted to wear one.

Plus, I cannot do a cartwheel, which I never even knew that I could not do before. And I am not speaking to Anya, even though she said that she was sorry three times. So this day has been like a huge, gigantic flop.

When I get home, Mom asks, "How was your day?" and I say, "Horrible," and she does not even ask why because the twins are drooling or pooping or crying or doing something else that is gross. So my day gets even worse.

I sit on my bed with my bag of gummy bears, but I do not even feel like eating one. I am reading the script that Mrs. Spangle gave me, and she is right: I have a *lot* of lines. And the lines have a lot of exclamation points, and I love exclamation points, which Natalie does not know how to read.

I get the tiniest bit more excited about being the narrator, and I try reading some of my lines out loud to myself.

"What you doing, Mandy?" Timmy wanders into my bedroom even though there is a sign on my door that says TIMMY with a gigantic *X* over his name.

I want to tell him to get out, but I also want to read my narrator lines to someone, so I am stuck between a rock and a rock. (Dad always says he is stuck between a rock and a hard place, which really makes no sense because a rock *is* hard. So I think it should be "stuck between a rock and a rock.")

I stuff my bag of gummy bears under my pillow before Timmy can see it.

"What does that sign on my door mean?" I ask.

"No Timmy," he answers, and he looks pretty

sad, actually. But I need to make sure he understands the rules if I am going to let him come into my room.

"Good," I say. "Now come listen to me practice my lines."

Timmy's eyes get real wide, and I think it is a little weird that he is so happy about me reading these narrator lines to him. Even if there are a lot of lines and I do read with expression.

Timmy does not come over right away, like he thinks I am playing a trick or something.

"Hurry up and come here," I tell him. "I am not asking, I am telling." I can say this to Timmy because Mom is not here to tell me not to.

Timmy crawls onto my bed and sits right next to me so our legs are touching, which I do not like. But I let him sit that way just so I can make sure he does not move and find my gummy bears by accident.

"I got a very gigantic part in the second-grade Presidential Pageant," I tell him, and Timmy looks at me like I am a big deal, which is exactly what I wanted. "You are not allowed to come." And then he looks sad again.

"But you will not really care, because I am going to practice my whole part for you now," I continue. "You have to be very quiet and never, ever talk. Or move. I need to concentrate. Okay?"

"Okay, Mandy," Timmy says, and sometimes he is not that bad for a three-year-old, I guess.

I read my whole part to Timmy one time and then another, and he stays very still and silent. When I am finished, he claps his hands for me, which I kind of like a lot.

"Close your eyes," I say. "I have a surprise." Timmy squeezes his eyes shut real tight and puts his hands over them. I reach under my pillow, open my gummy bear bag, and pull out one bear of each color. Then I stuff the bag back under my pillow before Timmy opens his eyes and sees its hiding spot.

"Hold out your hands, but don't open your eyes," I say, because I like to be in charge like a president. Timmy listens. I place the gummy bears into his hands, and they are warm and gooey from mine. "Open."

Timmy opens his eyes and he smiles real wide. "Thanks, Mandy!" he says, and I kind of almost like my brother right now, except not too much.

"Eat the red one last," I tell him. "Red is the best."

"Dinnertime, you two," Dad calls up the stairs, so Timmy sticks all the gummy bears in his mouth at once and starts chomping on them, which is not how I just said to eat them. I wrinkle up my nose and give him my "You are gross" face.

My family is supposed to eat dinner at the humongous oval table in our kitchen, but now it is always covered with twin stuff. So Mom makes Timmy and me eat at the picnic table in the toy room while she and Dad take care of the twins, which is the worst way ever to eat dinner. Because even if I kind of like Timmy today, I have already seen way too much of him. And plus, that picnic table is for babies.

"I am eight years old!" I call to my parents from the dumb picnic table.

"We know your age, Amanda," Dad answers. "Thanks for reminding us."

"I am too old to sit at a stupid kiddie table," I call back. "I am not a baby."

"Don't say 'stupid,'" Mom answers, because she is not a good listener about my problems.

I slouch down at the table and eat a couple of bites of chicken and all my macaroni and cheese. I rip the treetops off my pieces of broccoli but leave the trunks, and then I stand up to leave.

"I not done," Timmy says to me with a glob of macaroni and cheese hanging from his mouth.

"Chew faster," I tell him, and I carry all the food that I do not want to eat into the kitchen and put it in the trash before Mom or Dad can make me take five more bites of anything. I want to go practice my cartwheel because I cannot have Natalie able to do a cartwheel and me not. That is just humiliating.

Dad is sitting on the couch in the den, trying to get one of the twins to sleep.

"How do I learn a cartwheel?" I ask him.

"A cartwheel?"

"Yes," I say. "All the girls in second grade can do a cartwheel except me." I do not actually know if this is true, but it is close enough.

"Hmm," Dad says. "I don't know if I've ever done a cartwheel myself, but I think you need a lot of upper-body strength."

"What's that?"

"It means you need big arm muscles," Dad says. He holds out the arm that does not have the twin and tightens it so that his muscles stick out. "Why don't you drop and give me ten?"

"Ten what?" Dad makes no sense sometimes.

"Push-ups," he says. "Let me put Cody down, and I'll come back and show you." But I know that putting the twin down could take all night, and I do not have that kind of time if I am going to learn how to do a cartwheel before bed.

I walk over to Dad's dumbbell collection in the corner of the den. "Dumbbell" is a funny name, I think, because weights do not talk, so I do not understand how people know they are dumb. Maybe they are smart and have a mean name-call for no reason, like how Dennis calls me "Polka Dot" even though I stopped wearing the underwear.

Dad always lifts these weights to make his arm

muscles big, so I think this will be much faster than any push-up or whatever they are called.

I try to pick up one of the weights, but I cannot get it even with both of my hands. The next one is also too heavy, so I go all the way to the end of the rack for one of the smallest. I lift it up and hold it over my head with both hands, which is a lot harder than I think it should be, and I see why Dad's arm muscles are so big. I try to move the weight to only one hand so I can bring it down, and it slips.

It slips onto the floor and makes a huge crash.

It also almost hits my toe but does not, and no one is even happy that my foot is not broken when they come into the den to yell at me.

"Those weights are too heavy for you, Amanda!" Dad yells.

"You're going to wake the twins, Amanda!" Mom yells.

"At least I didn't break my toes!" I yell back,

and I stomp out of the room. I feel tears start to tickle the corners of my eyes for the second time today, but I push them back inside.

Because I may be only the narrator and I may not be able to do a cartwheel, but I, Mandy Berr, will never be a damp crybaby.

CHAPTER 7

Worst Audience Ever

I DO NOT TALK TO THE TWINS EVER.

I know that they do not talk—I am not a dope. But Mom and Dad always talk to them as if they are going to answer, which I think is silly, because what is the point?

But today Mrs. Spangle let the rest of the class practice their lines during school, and I did not get to practice once. She had lined up all the presidents in order and had them read their parts. They each have only eight lines, so I don't know why they have to practice so much. I have fifty-six lines altogether—I counted them—so if anyone should get to practice in front of everybody, it is me.

"You are the thread that holds the quilt together," Mrs. Spangle had said when I asked if it was my turn yet. "We need to get the squares all assembled and in order before we can sew them into one piece." And I do not know what she is talking about with this quilt, but I do know that I am not happy that I was sitting by myself for a whole hour and did not get to say one line.

So now here I am: a whole day with no practice and the most lines of anyone. I ask Timmy if he will listen to me read my lines again, but he does not want to, which I think is rude. He is three years old and should not have a say in what he gets to do. If I could make him throw up those gummy bears, I would take them back.

I want to read my lines to Mom, but she is in the laundry room, which is the loudest room in the whole house, and I do not feel like shouting. Dad is still at work, and I want to practice right this minute.

This leaves the twins. And I never talk to the twins.

The twins are sitting in their carriers on the kitchen table. They are not asleep, but they do not look very awake, either. They kind of look like globs, but they are the best that I have.

I stand in front of them and start to read, and they do not even open their eyes a little bit more to show that they are listening.

I read my lines with a lot of expression and everything, and I know that I am doing a good job, thank you very much. Plus, I am pretty funny about it, and the twins do not laugh once. I do not know if they even know how to laugh yet, but if anything should make them laugh, it is me.

"I don't need you twins!" I finally shout at them with my "You are driving me bananas" face. "I have a best friend who is a better listener." But then I remember that I am not speaking to Anya because of the cartwheel problem, and this makes me sad.

I will have to make up with Anya, I guess, or else I will have no one to read to. I am not so mad at her about the cartwheel problem anymore. And we sat together at lunch today, so maybe we are already made up. I just have to make sure.

I decide to call Anya's house right away, even though Mom does not like me to use the phone without her permission. This call is too important to wait. Plus, the twins are not crying, so I will be able to hear.

I dial Anya's number, and I am very good at remembering it.

"Hello?" Anya's mom answers.

"Hi, this is Mandy. Is Anya there, please?" I am super polite on the phone, and Mom should have no complaints.

"Just a minute, Mandy," and then I hear Anya's mom call her to the phone.

"Hello?" Anya answers.

"We're friends, right?"

"Mandy?"

"Yes."

"Yes, we're friends. Why?" Anya asks.

I let out a sigh, and I think I was maybe holding my breath this whole time. "Good. I thought you were still mad about the cartwheel problem."

"I wasn't mad. You were mad at me, remember?" she says.

"Oh. Yeah. Well, good, I'm not mad."

"Me neither."

"Can I practice my narrator part with you?

Mrs. Spangle didn't let me read it all day."

"I can't now, I have—"

"Amanda . . . ," I hear over my shoulder. Uh-oh.

I hang up on Anya real fast and hope that she will not be mad now, even though she was not mad before.

"I had to talk to Anya," I explain to Mom. "No one will listen to me practice my narrator lines for the Presidential Pageant."

"Narrator? I thought you were George Washington?" Mom asks. And then I feel a little bit hot on my forehead, because maybe I am wrong and George Washington is still the better part, even though he only has eight lines.

"Mrs. Spangle made me the narrator," I explain, keeping my eyes on the kitchen floor, which needs to be washed, I think. "She made Natalie George Washington."

"I'm sure you'll make a perfect narrator," Mom

tells me. "Don't you like even one thing about your part?"

"I have a lot of lines," I answer, because I do like having a lot of things, like lines and like gummy bears.

"That's great," Mom says. And I was not expecting this, if I am being honest.

"Really?"

"Of course," Mom says.

"Better than being George Washington?"

"I'm sure Natalie will do a great job too," Mom answers. "But I think you have the perfect part for you." And this makes me feel a little bit better about the whole George Washington thing.

"How about you practice your lines with me? I'm ready now," Mom says.

"But what about—?" I begin, and I look around for Timmy or laundry or a crying twin or something else that will make Mom not pay attention to me.

"Let me hear it," Mom says.

I begin to read my part, and I use a ton of expression and everything. And I get almost halfway finished before a twin starts to fuss.

"We'll have to continue later," Mom says. "Great job so far."

But I do not feel like stopping yet, so I keep practicing.

"Amanda, I have to take care of the twins," Mom interrupts me. "You need to stop for a while."

So I stomp my foot and cross my arms and yell, "I wish I were five years old!"

"Don't be so dramatic, Amanda," Mom says. "I'll listen to the rest of your lines after dinner." But dinner is forever away and I want to practice my lines now. "Do me a favor and go get the Packles' mail from next door. They're on vacation this week, and I said we would pick it up for them."

"No, thank you," I answer.

"Amanda," Mom says in her "This is your warning" voice. "I'm not asking, I'm telling."

I groan real loud like a dinosaur and stomp out of our house and across our front lawn to the Packles' mailbox. Inside, the box is stuffed with white envelopes and no magazines, which is the worst kind of mail because it does not even have any pictures. I march back to my house and throw the mail on the couch.

"Here's the stupid mail!" I yell super loud so Mom knows I have listened.

"Don't say 'stupid,' Amanda," Mom calls back. "And no yelling. Timmy is still taking his nap."

I pound up the stairs to my room. I had five whole years with no brother or sister, I remember, and those were the best years of my life. I think

Mom was a better listener then, though maybe she was not. I flop onto my bed and stare down at my Magic Mountain Wonderland. I wish I could live on the mountain for real, in one of the holes at the very top with all of the red bears. I would decorate it with Rainbow Sparkle wallpaper and periwinkle furniture, and I would eat dinner with the gummy bears every night, and not at some silly kiddie table either. I would watch TV whenever Rainbow Sparkle was on, and I would talk to Anya on the phone anytime I wanted, and my Magic Mountain Wonderland would be very quiet, except for when I made noise.

And Natalie would never, ever be invited over because she would do cartwheels and steal my George Washington parts and be no fun at all.

CHAPTER 8

The Break-In

I HAVE DECIDED THAT I AM absolutely positive that I cannot live in my house anymore. It is a whole week later, and no one listens to me except Rainbow Sparkle. I have not practiced my narrator lines all the way through with one family member—not ever—and this is just unfair.

It is not even that my house is so boring; it's just too loud. I like loud noises, but only when they are coming from me. Not from Timmy, not from the washing machine or the dishwasher or the microwave, and definitely not from the twins.

The Presidential Pageant is less than a week away now, and every single time I have tried to read all of my lines to Mom, someone has started crying, and it makes me too mad to try again. I cannot concentrate on practicing my fifty-six narrator lines with all this racket. "I am going outside," I call, and no one answers because nobody listens to me.

I go out our back door and stand on the side of the house where I will be alone, my script with Mrs. Spangle's yellow highlighting held tightly in my hands. I lean against the side of our house, but then I remember about the caterpillars and I stand up straight again. I bend my neck down to read, even though I remember most of my lines in my head because I have read them so much. It is too dark on the side of the house to see the words real good, though, and it is slowing me down.

I look toward the back door, but I definitely cannot go into that house again. In our driveway is a big pile of dirt and sticks that Dad is going to put on our flowers. I walk over to the edge of the pile and look up. The stack is a little bit smelly and much taller than me. It would make a good hill for sledding, only there is no snow.

This is when it hits me: This pile would also make a good Magic Mountain Wonderland—one that is much bigger and more special than the one in my bedroom, because it is a real mountain! I can build on it and live at the top like the red gummy bears. Or at least I can practice my lines up there and not have Timmy or the twins making noise and bothering me. All I have to do is create a staircase up the side of the pile, and then when I am at the top, I will be too high in the sky for anybody to reach me. It is the perfect plan, I think.

I put one foot in the bottom, and my sneaker

sinks in a little bit, but not too much. I kick my foot forward so I can make a step inside the dirt, and then I do the same thing with my other leg. I carve my own staircase in the side of my Magic Mountain, and I use my hands and knees to help keep my balance as I crawl up. Sticks and dirt scatter underneath me each time I move, but the mountain stays in place until I make it to the tippy-top. I sit down carefully because I am a little bit afraid, if I am being honest. The Magic Mountain Wonderland looks much higher from the top than from the bottom, but it is very quiet and it does not have Timmy or the twins.

"Wahoo!" I exclaim to myself, because I am president of Magic Mountain Wonderland.

I lift up my script to practice and it is covered in dirt, which I was not expecting, actually. It is a little hard for me to read. Each time I try to wipe the dirt off, my hand makes the paper even more smeary. I try to use my elbow, and then my knee, but they are covered with dirt too. This is a pretty big problem.

I cannot go back inside with all of this dirt on me, because Mom will take away more Rainbow Sparkle TV shows. I will need to clean up first, but Dad unhooked our outside hose after I gave Timmy a shower with it, so that is not an option.

I turn toward the Packles' house next door. The Packles are still on vacation, I know, because Mom keeps sending me to pick up their mail, so their house will be empty and I can use their bathroom. And maybe, just for a minute or two, I can pretend that it is my new place and I can make believe that their furniture is periwinkle.

I know where they keep their extra key. It is under a frog statue on their front porch, which seems like a pretty silly place to keep a key, if you ask me.

Carefully, I use the steps I carved to climb down from Magic Mountain Wonderland, and I walk over to the Packles' house, shaking off as much dirt as I can on the way. I walk onto their front porch, and right there, under the frog where I knew it would be, is their spare key. I lift it up, walk to their front door, and try to stick the key into the slot.

Nothing.

I jingle and jangle the key to try to make it fit, and it doesn't.

Now, I am not so good at opening locked things, so I do not know what I am supposed to do to make this work. I turn the key upside down, right-side up, to the left, to the right, and every which way in between. And the Packles' front door will not open.

My script, which I put right next to the frog so I could concentrate, is blowing in the breeze,

and I am afraid it is going to fly away, so I stick it under the frog. Then I return to the door, and I again try to put the key into the hole this way and that way.

"What are you doing, Amanda?!" I jump so high that I am surprised my head does not hit the ceiling of the Packles' porch. I turn around to find Dad's car in the street, Dad hanging halfway out of the driver's side window, staring at me.

"Nothing," I answer.

"Nothing?"

"Just checking on the frog," I say, which sounds like a dumb reason for being on the Packles' porch, even to me. I make sure to keep my hands—my dirty hands holding the Packles' key—behind my back so Dad cannot see.

"Get home right now," Dad says. "I want to talk to you."

I pull my script out from under the frog and

put the key back. Then I stomp over to my house and follow Dad through the garage.

"It is too loud in our house." I say each word like it is its own sentence, because I have decided that whatever I am going to be in trouble for is not my fault. It is Mom's fault and Timmy's fault and the twins' fault for being too loud, and since it is not Dad's fault yet, I need to explain this to him.

Dad turns and looks at me. "How did you get so dirty?"

"It is too loud in our house," I repeat, because Dad is not listening to my problem.

"Too loud for what?"

"I cannot practice my lines for the Presidential Pageant," I whine. "It's too loud, so I climbed on top of Magic Mountain Wonderland to practice my lines. But then I could not see them because my script had dirt on it. So I was going to the Packles' house to clean up. Because they are on vacation. I know this because Mom sent me to get their mail every day this week."

Dad looks at me with no words for a few seconds, because I have stumped him, I guess.

"You were going to break into their house?" Dad asks.

"No, I had a key," I say. "They keep it under their frog."

"You cannot go around the neighborhood breaking into people's houses, Amanda," Dad says.

"I wasn't breaking in—"

"Tim? Is that you?" Mom's head pokes out of the door. Dad's name is Tim, like Timmy without the "*my*." Although sometimes Grandmom calls Dad "Timmy" too, which I think is a silly name to call a grown-up.

"Be right in," Dad says. "Just finishing talking to Amanda." And he does not tattletale to Mom about the dirt and the Packles' frog and key, so that is something.

Mom goes back inside, and I cross my arms. Dad stares at me, and neither of us moves.

"Come here," Dad says, and we walk to the side of the house where the unhooked-up hose is. Dad screws the nozzle back onto the waterspout. "Put your script down somewhere safe," he says. I run and place my script by the bottom of my Magic Mountain Wonderland and return to Dad.

"Hold out your arms," he instructs. I do, and he squirts water from the hose right onto my hands and elbows. The water is pretty cold, but I do not say anything. Dad pours some water onto his own hands and dabs them across my cheeks, wiping off the dirt.

"Good," Dad says. "Now run into the garage and take your shoes and clothes off so you don't track any mulch into the house. Close the garage door so the neighbors won't see. I'll meet you in your room." I run to pick up my script and then into the garage. I press the button to close the door, and then I pull my shoes and pants and shirt off and leave them in a heap on the ground. I open the door to our house and run up the stairs in my underwear, which is not polka dot because I do not wear polka-dot underwear anymore.

I put on my purple nightgown, which is not quite periwinkle, but it is the closest I have. I sit on my bed and wait for Dad to come punish me. I do not even know what the big deal is, because this does not seem nearly as bad as the time that I threw Mom's keys in the oven because I did not want to go to the grocery store. The oven was not on or anything, but I still got into big-time trouble.

And plus, I wasn't going to take anything from the Packles' house. I only wanted a place to clean up, so I do not understand why Dad is flipping out.

I never even got inside, anyway, so I could not make believe that it was my own place, and that is the real tragedy.

Dad comes into my room many minutes later. I know it is many minutes because I have eaten most of my bag of gummy bears, and I am mad because I will not have lots left if he keeps me up here much longer.

"Did you think about why you cannot try to get into people's houses without asking?" Dad asks.

"Yes," I say, even though I have not.

"Good," he says. "It's been tough around here these past few months with the twins, huh?"

I nod.

"It'll get better when they're a little older, you know," Dad says. "They are going to adore you."

I nod again, because I think I am getting out of trouble. But not because I want the twins to adore me, because I do not care what the twins like.

"Do you want to finish practicing your lines for the assembly with me, right now before dinner?" Dad asks.

"Yes," I say. I think about giving Dad some gummy bears so he can eat them while I read, but it is probably not a good idea to let him know that they are in here.

"Let's hear it," Dad says, and he snuggles next to me on my bed, and I am happy for a little bit. I make it through half of my lines, and Dad laughs, and everything is great and dandy.

And then Dad rests his head on my pillow and hears the gummy bear bag crinkle underneath him. And this is a disaster, because Dad says, "You can't spoil your dinner with this candy" and takes the whole bag away.

And then nothing is great and dandy anymore.

CHAPTER 9

Teachers Old and New

MRS. SPANGLE IS PRETTY OLD, I think. I did not know this at first, because she has glasses, so I cannot really see if her eyes are crinkly. And her porcupine hair is very red—super-duper red like a clown's—so I cannot tell if it is white underneath like Grandmom's.

But today Mrs. Spangle tells us, "When I was born, John Kennedy was our president," and I am positive that John Kennedy was president a very, very long time ago.

"Wow, that was like one hundred years ago," I say, and Mrs. Spangle gives me a "This is your warning" look. But I do not know for certain if she is unhappy because I said she is one hundred years old or because I called out.

I clamp one hand over my mouth and raise the other one in the air.

"Yes, Mandy?" Mrs. Spangle calls on me.

"John Kennedy was president a hundred years ago, right?" I ask.

"He was president during the 1960s, not one hundred years ago," Mrs. Spangle says. "Boy, Mandy, you sure know how to make a teacher feel good."

And I do not know for sure, but I think Mrs. Spangle is kidding with me then.

Mrs. Spangle takes us to the cafeteria to practice the Presidential Pageant on the stage for the first time. She calls it a "dress rehearsal," which I think is silly because nobody is wearing a dress since it is Gym Day. She says that "dress rehearsal" just means that we will practice like we are performing the show for real. Everybody who has a prop as part of their costume is allowed to bring it, so Natalie grabs an old suit jacket and Dennis places a fake black mustache on his lip. They do not even have their real costumes on yet, and I am already upset. Mrs. Spangle had told all my classmates to dress up on the day of the assembly however they think their president would have looked.

"What costume should I wear?" I had asked, and I had raised my hand and everything.

Mrs. Spangle had told me, "You can wear whatever you like, Mandy," which is not the answer I wanted to hear.

I think it is only fair that if everybody else gets to wear a costume like they are going trick-or-treating, I should get to wear one too.

I told Mom that I wanted to wear my Rainbow

Sparkle costume from last Halloween, but she said that she does not think that is what Mrs. Spangle meant when she said I could wear whatever I want.

Natalie puts on her dad's suit jacket and pulls her dark hair into a low ponytail, and she does not look like George Washington one bit.

"Where is your white hair?" I ask. "You cannot be George Washington with no white hair."

"My mom is making me a wig out of felt," Natalie answers. "But it's not ready yet." And I do not say anything then because I would like to have a wig made out of felt too.

I would also like to have a fake mustache like Dennis, even though Dennis cannot keep his mustache on his lip. If I could wear a fake mustache, I would know how to keep it on, but Dennis's is always on the ground, and I think this is a waste of a good mustache.

We get to practice with a microphone for the

first time, and that is pretty exciting because I love microphones. I had a toy microphone once, but then Dad hid it because he said he was getting a headache.

Mrs. Spangle has placed metal folding chairs in a line across the stage for us to sit on until it is our turn. Luckily, it is my turn a lot, so I do not have to sit too much. Also, I get to speak first, even though I am not George Washington, so I am pretty happy about that, too.

When I step up to the microphone for the first time, I put my mouth real close to it. "Four score and—"

"Step back, Mandy," Mrs. Spangle interrupts me, which I do not think you are supposed to do during a dress rehearsal.

I take a step back and then lean my face forward until my mouth is super close to the microphone again.

"Four score and—"

"Move your face away from the microphone, Mandy."

I move back, even though I do not think Mrs. Spangle knows how to use a microphone right.

"Four score and—"

"Perfect."

Natalie's part is right after my opening, which is not fun because this means she has to sit next to me onstage and we have nothing to talk about. Mrs. Spangle says we should not be talking onstage anyway, and I do not get a warning from her once during our dress rehearsal because Natalie is excellent at not getting in trouble.

What Natalie is not excellent at doing is exclaiming, so she reads her George Washington lines like a robot, even though she has memorized her whole part and gets every word correct. When she finishes and returns to her seat next to me, I do not tell her that she did a good job because she didn't.

The rest of our dress rehearsal goes pretty well—although Dennis's mustache falls to the ground three more times, so that is not great.

I think that it will be a good assembly, but I think it could be even better if Mrs. Spangle would let me stand closer to the microphone.

CHAPTER 10

Hail to Mandy

IT IS THE DAY OF THE BIG SECOND–GRADE Presidential Pageant, and I am a bit nervous. After all, Mrs. Spangle said that I have the most important part in the whole show.

Mom bought me a new outfit to wear for the assembly, but she will not let me see it until right before I get dressed. I think this is a bad idea, because what if I hate it? But Mom says that it is a surprise.

"You won't hate it, Amanda," she says, but I

do not know how she knows this for sure.

I wake up early because I feel very jumpy. I decide to practice all my lines one more time so that I will say them extra good at the assembly. I guess I am saying them super loud, though, because Mom barges in my room real fast when I am not even halfway through the show.

"It's good that you are practicing one more time," she says. "But maybe you could do it a little quieter so you don't wake your brothers and sister."

And I do not know how she thinks I am going to read with expression when I have to be quiet, but I try my best anyway, because Mom stays in my room to watch me.

"You are going to do a great job today," Mom says. "Dad and I can't wait to see you."

"And no twins, right?" I want to make sure.

"Nope, Grandmom is coming over to watch them, so it will just be us."

"Good." I nod real hard so she knows that I mean it.

"Are you ready to see your new outfit?" Mom asks.

"Does it have fancy-dancy periwinkle sunglasses?"

"You can't wear sunglasses at your Presidential Pageant, even if you are a star," Mom says. "Let me go get it." She pops out of the room and comes back with a hanger dripping in plastic. I rip the plastic off as fast as I can, and there it is: the most perfect, gorgeous periwinkle dress I have ever seen.

"Wahoo!" I throw my arms around Mom's neck tightly. "Best dress ever."

"And real periwinkle, right?" Mom says. She looks pretty happy with herself.

"Yep." I run to my box of 152 crayons and pull out the periwinkle one just to be sure. This crayon is the shortest in the box because I use it so much. I hold it up to the dress, and it matches exactly, and I have never been so happy in my life.

Mom helps me put the dress on because it has a lot of snaggy zippers and finger-pinching buttons. She brushes my hair real straight, and I think it is still a little bit shiny from the sugar.

"Can I wear my Rainbow Sparkle headband?" I ask. It is a white headband with purple gemstones on it, and it matches my dress like a pair of mittens match each other. It is not a pair of fancy-dancy periwinkle sunglasses, but it is pretty close, I think.

"I don't see why not," Mom says, and I push my hair back with the headband. I look at myself in the mirror, and I am almost perfect.

"I'm going to make you a big breakfast," Mom says, "so you'll have lots of strength for your performance." She shuffles out of my room quietly, and I pull open my underwear drawer as soon as she leaves. As quickly as possible, I change out of my white underwear and into my favorite polka-dot pair, even though I said that I would never wear them again. I am pretty sure you cannot see through my periwinkle dress, so I will be safe. And also, they will bring me good luck, I think.

Now I look perfect, and I do not even feel so nervous and jumpy anymore.

Anya does not say one thing about my dress when she sees me at school, so I have to say, "Don't you love my dress?" so she knows she is supposed to. She says that she does, and I tell her I like hers, too, even though it is white and I hate white dresses. I am very polite, I think.

Everyone looks pretty excited, and even Mrs. Spangle looks like she is not one hundred years old. The only person who looks miserable is Natalie.

Natalie looks like she is going to throw up, actually. And I can't have her throwing up on my new periwinkle dress when we are onstage. No way! I will need to put a stop to this throwing-up face right away.

"Here is a rule: No throwing up on my dress," I say to Natalie, and she clamps her lips together like she is a fish and looks at me like I have a monkey head.

"Huh?" I do not know why she can't understand what I am saying because I am very clear about the "No throwing up" rule.

"If you are going to throw up onstage, turn away from my dress, please," I repeat. "It is new."

"I'm not going to throw up," Natalie says.

"You look like you are wearing a throw-up face," I tell her. Her cheeks are as white as her George Washington wig, which I kind of want to try on, but I know Natalie will not let me because she never lets me try on her glasses.

Natalie shakes her head. "I just feel . . . ," She does not finish, which should not be allowed, because I do not know if she feels like she is going to be sick on my dress any minute.

"Feel what?"

"I'm nervous," Natalie tells me. And this is a big surprise to me, because Natalie does not seem like the jumpy type. "Aren't you nervous? You have so many lines."

"I'm not nervous," I tell her. "You want to know why?"

"Why?"

I lean in close to Natalie's ear and pull up one side of her George Washington wig, just to make sure she can hear me real good. "I am wearing my polka-dot underwear," I confess. And Natalie's eyes get real big then, like I have told her something ridiculous.

And then Natalie starts laughing very loud, which startles me so much that I jump way up in the air because I have never, ever heard Natalie laugh.

"They are good luck, I think," I tell her. "Because I was nervous like you this morning, but now I am not." And this makes Natalie laugh even more, which I would think was rude if I did not like to hear her laughing. Natalie thinks I am funny, which is kind of fantastic because Natalie is not a giggly person at all.

"So if you get scared onstage, just look at me," I tell Natalie. "And you will know what I am thinking about."

"What?" Natalie stops laughing for only one second.

"Polka-dot underwear," I whisper this part, too, so that Freckle Face Dennis cannot hear, because he is not part of the joke.

"I will. Thank you, Mandy," Natalie says. "I feel much better now."

"And no throw up on my dress, right?"

"Nope, I promise," she says.

We get in line to go to our big Presidential Pageant, and I am happy to stand next to Natalie even though she is not Anya. I do not care anymore that Natalie gets to be George Washington and to wear that big fluffy wig, because I am the narrator, and that is a very important part.

Plus, that wig is white, and white things do not go with polka dots.

When my classmates and I take the stage, they are all dressed up in costumes to look like their presidents, but I am the only one who gets to wear a brand-new periwinkle dress. I take my seat in the line of chairs across the stage, and I sit in the first one because I get to speak earliest.

Because Mrs. Spangle is right: The narrator is the thread that holds the quilt together.

Mrs. Spangle thanks all the parents for coming, and I do not pay much attention, if I am being honest. Because I want to get to the microphone and do my part right away. Finally I hear the parents applauding, and Mrs. Spangle looks at me so I know it is my turn.

I approach the microphone but do not put my mouth on it, just like Mrs. Spangle said. I take a deep breath, and I begin.

In my grandest, loudest, most expressive voice, I say, "Four score and seven years ago . . ."

The audience smiles huge grins at me, and I see Mom and Dad smiling the biggest. I finish my first part, and Natalie steps up to the microphone behind me.

"Remember to exclaim," I whisper in her ear as I go back to my seat. And even though Natalie does not let out one "Wahoo!" she is pretty good at being George Washington because she is very serious. And I guess George Washington really was a serious president, so maybe it is a good fit.

Plus, if I were George Washington, I would not have gotten my new periwinkle dress, which is my new favorite dress in the whole world, so the narrator is the perfect part for me. It looks like Mrs. Spangle was right all along, even if she is pretty old (and I will not talk about her being one hundred years old anymore, I've decided).

Dennis walks up to the microphone in his Teddy Roosevelt vest and mustache, and he even combed his hair out of his Mohawk. "Nature is the place—" he begins in a loud, booming voice, and his mustache flies off of his lip, flutters through the air, and drops off the stage. Dennis does not keep speaking because he is shocked, I think.

"Nature is the place . . . ," Mrs. Spangle coaches him from the side of the stage, but Dennis stays silent. He is going to ruin our Presidential Pageant because he has a lost mustache.

Before Mrs. Spangle can tell me not to, I pop up from my seat real fast, run down the steps on the side of the stage, and pick Dennis's mustache up from the first row. Fast as a cat, I am back on stage by the microphone, and I hand Dennis his mustache.

And he looks pretty surprised, actually.

"Here, Freckle Face," I whisper, standing far away from the microphone so that no one else will hear.

"Thanks, Mandy," Dennis answers, and I cannot believe that he called me my real name and not "Polka Dot." He takes the mustache from my hand and sticks it back on his lip, and he holds it there the whole time as he finishes his Teddy

Roosevelt part. The audience gives him a big round of applause when he is finished, even though I am the one who saved his mustache.

Each time I get up to speak, I am better and better, if I do say so myself. But the rest of my class is pretty good too. When our show is over, we stand at the front of the stage and hold hands in a long line. We bow one time and then another, and the audience claps and claps, and I have never been so happy in my life.

"You made a great narrator, Mandy," Natalie says to me as we walk down the stairs on the side of the stage. And I thank her like I really mean it.

"You were a pretty good George Washington too," I tell her, and I am not just being polite. "Maybe sometime I could try on your wig?" I think she could let me try it on since I taught her how to not throw up and all.

"You could come over to my house this weekend?" Natalie suggests, and I say this is a good idea. Because I think getting to wear a George Washington wig is worth going over to Natalie's house.

"Do you like Rainbow Sparkle's TV show?" I ask her.

"I've never seen it." Natalie looks down at the floor. "My mom doesn't let me watch TV."

"That is a tragedy," I tell her. "Only not really, because—ta-da!—you will come over my house and we will watch Rainbow Sparkle together. Just make sure you bring your wig." And Natalie grins so much when I say this that I think her face might explode like a bubblegum bubble.

"Maybe you could try on my George Washington wig and my glasses at the same time," Natalie suggests, and I tell her that this is the best idea I have heard all day.

"Mandy!" I hear someone call behind me in a voice that sounds like Mom's. But she never, ever calls me "Mandy" so I am super-duper confused.

When I turn around, Mom and Dad almost walk right into me, and they are smiling as big as Natalie.

"You were amazing, Mandy," Mom says. "The best narrator I've ever seen."

"Hey, you called me 'Mandy'!" I say this with a lot of exclaim because it is the new best thing I've heard all day.

"If that's what you like, that's your name," Mom says, and she is being a good listener. First the dress, then the headband, now my name, so I give her a big hug.

"I'm so proud of all your hard work," Dad says. "That was a lot of speaking you had to do."

I agree that it was, and my parents take my picture on the stage by the microphone so I can always remember the time that I was the best narrator ever.

"Nice job, Polka Dot," Dennis says to me, almost like he is a nice person. "Thank you for helping with my mustache."

"No problem, Freckle Face," I say, and Dennis

does not even stick his tongue out at me then. This might be the first time that I do not think Dennis is horrible.

Anya gives me a squishy hug, because she is wearing a pillow to look round like President Taft, and it is just about the best hug ever. I wave good-bye to Natalie, and she points to her wig and gives me a thumbs-up.

Natalie is maybe not so boring, I think.

"I knew you would make a great narrator, Mandy," Mrs. Spangle tells me. "No one reads with expression like you." Mom wants to take my picture with Mrs. Spangle, so my teacher leans down low so I can throw my arm over her shoulders. I smile real wide, because I am in my periwinkle dress and because I am not angry with Mrs. Spangle for not making me George Washington anymore. She may even be one of my favorite people in the world, at least most of the time.

After we leave, Mom and Dad take me to have ice cream all by myself, with no Timmy and no twins. I can barely lick the scoops into my mouth because I am grinning so much.

"Wahoo!" I call out when I am in the middle of my ice-cream cone, because sometimes a "wahoo" is just needed.

"So what was the best part of your day, Mandy?" Mom asks, and I think real hard because it is a very important question.

"I have three," I finally answer. "My new beautiful periwinkle dress, me being the best narrator ever, and this."

"The ice cream?" Dad asks.

"No," I say. "This." I circle my hand around the three of us because I am glad we are together.

And I am glad Timmy and the twins are not here, but that would not sound nice, so I do not say it out loud.

"Me too," Mom says.

"And me three," Dad says. "By the way, I have something for you." And I cannot believe he spent all this time having a present and not giving it to me.

"Mandy's very own gummy bears," Dad says, and he hands me the most gigantic bag of bears I have ever seen. "All for you, as long as you promise not to hide them in your room. Deal?"

"Deal!" I answer, even though I cannot absolutely promise that, because sometimes a gummy bear hiding place is just needed.

"How about," Mom says, "you do your narrator part for Grandmom and Timmy when we get home? I'm sure they would love to hear it."

"Only if I get to play all the parts," I say. "*All* of them."

"You got it." Dad laughs at me. "You still want to be president, huh?"

I nod real fast. Because I want to be in charge

like the presidents, of course, but that is not the real reason.

The real reason is that I want to be the first president ever to wear a periwinkle dress, a Rainbow Sparkle headband, and a pair of polka-dot underwear.

Mandy's Lessons:

1. DON'T WEAR POLKA-DOT UNDERWEAR WITH WHITE PANTS.
2. ALWAYS HAVE A BAG OF GUMMY BEARS AVAILABLE.
3. NEVER SQUEEZE CATERPILLARS LIKE GUMMY BEARS.
4. SUGAR DOES NOT BELONG IN HAIR, EVEN IF GEORGE WASHINGTON DID IT.
5. DON'T SAY YOU CAN DO A CARTWHEEL IF YOU CAN'T.
6. DUMBBELLS ARE HEAVY. AND ALSO DUMB.
7. BABIES HAVE NO SENSE OF HUMOR.
8. IT'S NOT NICE TO TAKE YOUR NEIGHBORS' KEYS WITHOUT ASKING.
9. TEACHERS DON'T LIKE TO BE CALLED "OLD."
10. NOT EVERYBODY GETS TO BE PRESIDENT.

READ ON FOR MANDY'S NEXT ADVENTURE!

The Pizza Problem

THE CENTER OF OUR PIZZA PIE IS MISSING because Dad is no good at giving directions.

The best part of a pizza slice is the first bite because the point is skinny and it is mouth-size and it never has any crust. Crust is useless because it has no cheese. I always try to make my brother Timmy eat my crust so that he will give me his first bite points. Mom says this is not allowed, but Dad does not because he is no good at giving directions.

Dad is also not a very good babysitter, if I am being honest. If he were, he would have said, *Mandy, do not touch the pizza until I come back.* Instead, Dad left me alone in the kitchen with the big, steamy pizza pie box, and he ran off to the twins' room.

One of the twins had started crying, because the twins are always crying, and I knew waiting for Dad to give me a slice could take all night. So I opened the pizza box, lifted the slices one by one, and bit off each delicious point before plopping the rest of the slice back in the box.

It was the best pizza pie I have ever had.

Only Dad does not think so, because when he comes back into the kitchen with a crying twin and sees the center of the pizza missing, his face turns as red as a tomato. He looks over at me slowly, so I cross my arms and stomp my foot and yell, "I had no dinner!" before he can say one word.

Dad turns away from me, digs through the twins' diaper bag, and walks back toward the twins' room with a package of wipes in his hand.

"Follow me," he calls over his shoulder. I keep my arms crossed and drag my heels on the kitchen floor.

"I had no dinner!" I repeat when we get to the twins' doorway.

"You need to learn to be patient, Mandy," Dad says. "Even Timmy did not take bites out of all of the pizza slices, and he's only three. You're eight—you should know better." And this makes me angry because I know I am better than Timmy, which is why Timmy is hungry right now and I am not.

"You are a bad babysitter," I inform Dad. "I am going to tell Mom on you." Dad laughs, which I think is rude.

"And what are you going to tell her?" Dad asks.

He begins changing the diaper of one of the twins, which is smelly and awful, so I hold my nose shut.

"Yow dow nawt ghive guwd dewektons," I answer.

"What?"

"Yow dow nawt ghive guwd dewektons," I repeat.

"I can't understand you when you're holding your nose," Dad says.

I whip my hand away from my face and yell, "YOU DO NOT GIVE GOOD DIRECTIONS!" real fast, and I guess I say it pretty loud, because the twin starts to cry again.

"Mandy," Dad begins in his "This is your warning" voice. "I think you should come here and help me change Samantha's diaper."

"No, thank you," I answer, and I am polite and everything.

"It's not a choice, Amanda," Dad says, and

I know that he means business. Dad only calls me "Amanda" when I am about to be in trouble, because he knows that I hate it.

I sigh a big puff of breath and shuffle over to the twins' changing table. I put one hand over my nose and my other hand over the twin's mouth and say, "Stop crying," which I think is pretty helpful.

"Mandy, no!" Dad pulls my hand away from the twin. "You can't cover her mouth like that— she won't be able to breathe."

"Then what do you want me to do?" I stomp my foot again. I would like to go up to my room and be in trouble by myself, but I stay put because I do not want to make Dad call me "Amanda" again.

"Here." Dad fastens the twin's new diaper and picks her up under the armpits. "Play with Samantha until I finish changing Cody. See if you can get her to stop crying."

I stare at Dad over the hand that is still covering my nose. I never, ever hold the twins because they are damp and gross and no fun at all. Dad looks back at me, neither of us moving, and the twin continues to howl.

"Amanda," Dad says, "either you play with Samantha right now or no Rainbow Sparkle TV show for—"

"Fine." I whip my hand away from my nose and reach out for the twin, because I am not having Rainbow Sparkle taken away from me again. No way! I wrap my arms around the twin like she is a pile of dirty clothes, and I sit on the floor.

"Here is a deal," I say to her. "You will stop crying right now, and I will tell you the secret about pizza." I lay the twin on the floor because I do not like damp things in my hands, and she almost starts being quiet.

"See? Your sister likes when you talk to her," Dad says as he spreads the other twin out on the changing table. But I do not answer him because I do not care what the twins like.

"The secret about pizza is that the points are the best part. The crust is the worst, because there is no cheese, but the best part is the first bite of a slice. And also, the best color in the whole world is periwinkle." I look up at Dad. "Am I done?" The twin is not crying anymore, so it only seems fair.

"No, now play with Cody while I—"

"Anybody home?" Mom calls from the living room. I dart out of the twins' room and run to her so I can tattle on Dad. She and Grandmom are piling shopping bags on our couch.

"Abracadabra!" Timmy runs down the stairs and leaps over the last three steps, landing with a thud next to the front door.

"Timmy!" Mom yells as he picks himself up. "What did I tell you about jumping off of the stairs? You're going to break a bone."

"Sorry," Timmy answers, and he tries to climb Grandmom like a jungle gym until she scoops him into her arms. He gives her a slobbery kiss.

"Yuck," I call.

"Hi, Mandy," Grandmom greets me as Timmy slinks down her body like a snake.

"Did you get me gummy bears?" I ask. Grandmoms are the best people for giving gummy bears because moms and dads usually say no.

"Not even a hello first?" Grandmom asks. "Come give me some sugar." Grandmom says to "give her sugar" when she wants a kiss, which is pretty silly, I think. Even if I am the sweetest person in my family, I would be sweeter if I had gummy bears first.

I kiss Grandmom on the lips, and I am not as

slobbery as Timmy about it. "How about those bears?" I ask again.

"Not today," Grandmom says. "Maybe next time." But next time is not helpful at all when I want gummy bears now.

"Well, how about my fancy-dancy periwinkle sunglasses?" I ask. I have wanted fancy-dancy periwinkle sunglasses for my whole entire life and still do not have any, so every time Mom and Grandmom go shopping, I ask them to buy me a pair.

"Mandy," Mom says, "no more B-R-A-T behavior, please."

"Why are we spelling?" Grandmom whispers to Mom, like she thinks I cannot hear anything.

"Because Timmy is a brat," I answer.

"Brat!" Timmy repeats, and he looks pretty proud of himself.

Mom rolls her eyes up to the ceiling and looks

at Grandmom. "That's why." She points to Timmy. "And, Mandy, don't call your brother a B-R-A-T."

"But—," I begin, but Mom interrupts me because she is never a good listener about my problems.

"Help me carry these bags of change into the laundry room, please," she says, picking up a pillowcase, which clinks and clanks as she swings it back and forth.

"Why do you have bags of change?" I ask.

"Your mom's taking them to the bank to put them in the magic coin machine for me," Grandmom explains. "It will turn the coins into dollar bills."

"It's magic?" Timmy asks excitedly.

"No, stupid," I say, even though I am not completely sure.

"Mandy!" Mom yells from the laundry room. "No S-T-U-P-I-D talk either."

"When you get the dollars, are you going to buy me my fancy-dancy periwinkle sunglasses?" I ask Grandmom.

"We'll see," Grandmom answers, which means "no" in grown-up talk. "I think you would enjoy those sunglasses even more if you bought them yourself. Don't you think?"

"I have no dollars," I answer, because that is the truth.

"You get an allowance, don't you?"

"Yes, but that is only two quarters," I explain. "No dollars."

"Then save up your quarters until you can take them to the magic coin machine and exchange them for dollars," Grandmom suggests. "When you have enough, you can buy the fancy-dancy sunglasses yourself."

"Periwinkle," I add.

"What?"

"You forgot 'periwinkle.' They are fancy-dancy periwinkle sunglasses," I explain.

"Right," Grandmom answers, and she pats me on the head like I am a dog. "Now come help your mother with these bags."

I sling a pillowcase over my shoulder, and it is very heavy. I lug it slowly to the laundry room.

"Right there on the floor, next to the others," Mom instructs, pointing. I dump the pillowcase on the floor with a crash, and this noise makes the twins start crying again.

"Mandy, be careful!" Mom calls from the kitchen, and I stick my tongue out because she is not here to see. I hear Grandmom and Dad in the twins' room trying to make them stop crying, so I sit on the floor of the laundry room because I do not want to talk to the twins again. I place my hands in one of the pillowcases and lift a humongous handful of coins in the air. I release them and let them sprinkle back into the pile, tinkling like raindrops.

There must be thousands and millions of coins in these bags—more than enough to buy my fancy-dancy periwinkle sunglasses.

"Tim, what happened to this pizza?" I hear Mom yell from the kitchen, and then I remember that I forgot to tell on Dad for being no good at giving directions.

"Ask Mandy," Dad calls back, so I leap to my feet real fast to close the laundry room door. I do not feel like talking about pizza points right now. Not when I have to figure out how to collect enough coins to buy my very own pair of fancy-dancy periwinkle sunglasses.

And maybe my own pizza, too.